To Lauren
From Grandmother + Granddaddy Henry
Happy 1st Birthday! August '81

Nicola Bayley's Book of
NURSERY RHYMES

Alfred A. Knopf · New York

For Elizabeth and William

Illustrations Copyright © 1975   by Nicola Bayley

All rights reserved under International and Pan-American
Copyright Conventions. Published in the United States
by Alfred A. Knopf, Inc., New York. Distributed by Ran-
dom House, Inc., New York. Originally published in
Great Britain by Jonathan Cape Ltd., London.

Printed in Italy

Library of Congress Cataloging in Publication Data
Main entry under title: Nicola Bayley's Book of
nursery rhymes. SUMMARY: Color drawings
accompany a collection of well-known nursery rhymes.
1. Nursery rhymes. [1. Nursery rhymes]
I. Bayley, Nicola. II. Title: Book of nursery rhymes.
PZ8.3.N536 1977   398.8   76-57923
ISBN 0-394-83561-1   ISBN 0-394-93561-6 lib. bdg.

BAA, baa, black sheep,
Have you any wool?
Yes sir, yes sir,
Three bags full;
One for the master,
And one for the dame,
And one for the little boy
Who lives down the lane.

WHO killed Cock Robin?
I, said the Sparrow,
With my bow and arrow,
I killed Cock Robin.

Who saw him die?
I, said the Fly,
With my little eye,
I saw him die.

Who caught his blood?
I, said the Fish,
With my little dish,
I caught his blood.

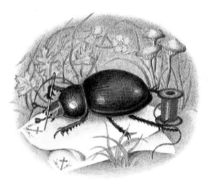

Who'll make his shroud?
I, said the Beetle,
With my thread and needle,
I'll make his shroud.

Who'll dig his grave?
I, said the Owl,
With my pick and shovel,
I'll dig his grave.

Who'll be the parson?
I, said the Rook,
With my little book,
I'll be the parson.

Who'll be the clerk?
I, said the Lark,
If it's not in the dark,
I'll be the clerk.

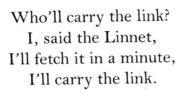

Who'll carry the link?
I, said the Linnet,
I'll fetch it in a minute,
I'll carry the link.

Who'll be chief mourner?
I, said the Dove,
I mourn for my love,
I'll be chief mourner.

Who'll carry the coffin?
I, said the Kite,
If it's not through the night,
I'll carry the coffin.

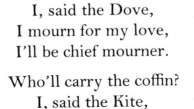

Who'll bear the pall?
We, said the Wren,
Both the cock and the hen,
We'll bear the pall.

Who'll sing a psalm?
I, said the Thrush,
As I sit on a bush,
I'll sing a psalm.

Who'll toll the bell?
I, said the Bull,
Because I can pull,
So Cock Robin, farewell.

All the birds of the air
Fell a-sighing and a-sobbing,
When they heard the bell toll
For poor Cock Robin.

MARY, Mary, quite contrary,
  How does your garden grow?
With silver bells and cockle shells
And pretty maids all in a row.

GOOSEY, goosey, gander,
　Whither shall I wander?
Upstairs and downstairs
And in my lady's chamber.
There I met an old man
Who would not say his prayers,
I took him by the left leg
And threw him down the stairs.

OLD Mother Hubbard
     Went to the cupboard,
To fetch her poor dog a bone;
     But when she came there
     The cupboard was bare
And so the poor dog had none.

She went to the baker's
     To buy him some bread;
But when she came back
     The poor dog was dead.

She went to the undertaker's
     To buy him a coffin;
But when she came back
     The poor dog was laughing.

She took a clean dish
     To get him some tripe;
But when she came back
     He was smoking a pipe.

She went to the alehouse
     To get him some beer;
But when she came back
     The dog sat in a chair.

She went to the tavern
     For white wine and red;
But when she came back
     The dog stood on his head.

She went to the fruiterer's
     To buy him some fruit;
But when she came back
     He was playing the flute.

She went to the tailor's
To buy him a coat;
But when she came back
He was riding a goat.

She went to the hatter's
To buy him a hat;
But when she came back
He was feeding the cat.

She went to the barber's
To buy him a wig;
But when she came back
He was dancing a jig.

She went to the cobbler's
To buy him some shoes;
But when she came back
He was reading the news.

She went to the seamstress
To buy him some linen;
But when she came back
The dog was a-spinning.

She went to the hosier's
To buy him some hose;
But when she came back
He was dressed in his clothes.

The dame made a curtsy,
The dog made a bow;
The dame said, Your servant,
The dog said, Bow-wow.

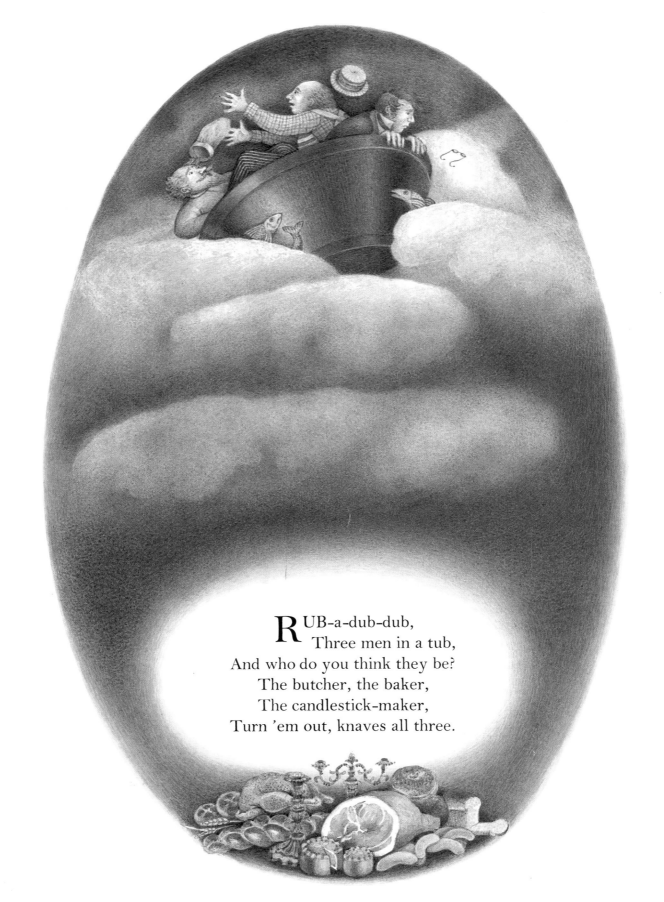

R UB-a-dub-dub,
   Three men in a tub,
And who do you think they be?
The butcher, the baker,
The candlestick-maker,
Turn 'em out, knaves all three.

DOCTOR Foster went to Gloucester
In a shower of rain;
He stepped in a puddle
Right up to his middle,
And never went there again.

AS I was going to St Ives,
I met a man with seven wives.
Each wife had seven sacks,
Each sack had seven cats,
Each cat had seven kits:
Kits, cats, sacks, and wives,
How many were there going to St Ives?

The Queen of Hearts she made some tarts
All on a summer's day;
The Knave of Hearts he stole those tarts
And took them quite away.

SING a song of sixpence,
A pocket full of rye;
Four and twenty blackbirds
Baked in a pie.

When the pie was opened,
The birds began to sing;
Was not that a dainty dish
To set before the King?

The King was in his counting-house,
Counting out his money;

The Queen was in the parlour,
Eating bread and honey.

The maid was in the garden,
Hanging out the clothes,
Along came a blackbird
And snapped off her nose.

SIMPLE Simon met a pieman
    Going to the fair;
Says Simple Simon to the pieman,
    Let me taste your ware.

Says the pieman to Simple Simon,
    Show me first your penny;
Says Simple Simon to the pieman,
    Indeed I have not any.

Simple Simon went a-fishing
    For to catch a whale;
All the water he had got
    Was in his mother's pail.

Simple Simon went a-hunting
    For to catch a hare;
He rode a goat about the streets,
    But couldn't find one there.

He went to catch a dickey bird,
    And thought he could not fail,
Because he'd got a little salt
    To put upon its tail.

He went to shoot a wild duck,
    But wild duck flew away;
Says Simon, I can't hit him
    Because he will not stay.

He went to ride a spotted cow,
    That had a little calf;
She threw him down upon the ground,
    Which made the people laugh.

Once Simon made a great snowball
    And brought it in to roast;
He laid it down before the fire
    And soon the ball was lost.

He went to try if cherries ripe
    Did grow upon a thistle;
He pricked his finger very much,
    Which made poor Simon whistle.

He went for water in a sieve,
    But soon it all ran through;
And now poor Simple Simon
    Bids you all adieu.

THERE was an old woman
     Who lived in a shoe,
She had so many children
     She didn't know what to do;
She gave them some broth
     Without any bread,
And whipped them all soundly
     And put them to bed.

THERE was a crooked man,
    And he walked a crooked mile,
He found a crooked sixpence
    Against a crooked stile;
He bought a crooked cat,
    Which caught a crooked mouse,
And they all lived together
    In a little crooked house.

MONDAY'S child
is fair of face,

Tuesday's child
is full of grace,

Wednesday's child
is full of woe,

Thursday's child
has far to go,

Friday's child
is loving and giving,

Saturday's child
works hard for a living,

And the child that is born on the Sabbath Day
Is bonny and blithe and good and gay.

HUMPTY Dumpty sat on a wall,
Humpty Dumpty had a great fall;
All the King's horses
And all the King's men
Couldn't put Humpty together again.

THREE blind mice, see how they run!
They all ran after the farmer's wife,
Who cut off their tails with a carving knife,
Did you ever see such a thing in your life
As three blind mice?

O NE, two,
Buckle my shoe;

Three, four,
Knock at the door;

Five, six,
Pick up sticks;

Seven, eight,
Lay them straight;

Nine, ten,
A big fat hen;

Eleven, twelve,
Dig and delve;

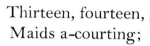

Thirteen, fourteen,
Maids a-courting;

Fifteen, sixteen,
Maids in the kitchen;

Seventeen, eighteen,
Maids in waiting;

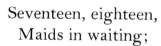

Nineteen, twenty,
My plate's empty.

LITTLE Miss Muffet
Sat on a tuffet,
Eating her curds and whey;
There came a big spider
Who sat down beside her
And frightened Miss Muffet away.

LITTLE Jack Horner
Sat in a corner
Eating a Christmas pie;
He put in his thumb
And pulled out a plum
And said, 'What a good boy am I!'

HEY diddle diddle, the cat and the fiddle,
    The cow jumped over the moon;
The little dog laughed
    To see such sport,
And the dish ran away with the spoon.

OLD King Cole was a merry old soul,
And a merry old soul was he;
He called for his pipe,
And he called for his bowl,
And he called for his fiddlers three.

THIS little pig went to market,
This little pig stayed at home,
This little pig had roast beef,
And this little pig had none,
And this little pig went wee-wee-wee
all the way home.